No Time to Nap

Heyday Books, founded in 1974, works to deepen people's
understanding and appreciation of the cultural, artistic,
historic, and natural resources of California and the
American West. It operates under a 501(c)(3) nonprofit
educational organization (Heyday Institute) and, in
addition to publishing books, sponsors a wide range of
programs, outreach, and events.

To help support Heyday or to learn more about us, visit
our website at www.heydaybooks.com, or write to us at
the address below.

Orders, inquiries, and correspondence should be
addressed to:
  Heyday Books
  P. O. Box 9145, Berkeley, CA 94709
  (510) 549-3564, Fax (510) 549-1889
  www.heydaybooks.com

Book design by Rebecca LeGates
Printed in China by Oceanic Graphic Printing, Inc.

10 9 8 7 6 5 4 3 2 1

GREAT
VALLEY

*The publishers wish to thank the James Irvine Foundation
for a grant that allowed us to publish this book as part of
our Great Valley series.*

Library of Congress Cataloging-in-Publication Data
Madison, Mike, 1947–
  No time to nap / Mike Madison ; illustrated by Mary
Peterson.
    p. cm.
  Summary: Looks at the "To Do" list of a very busy
farmer in California's central valley.
  ISBN 1-59714-046-5 (hardback : alk. paper)
  [1. Farm life—Fiction. 2. California—Fiction.] I.
Peterson, Mary, ill. II. Title.
  PZ7.M26513No 2007
  [E]—dc22
                                            2006020177

To Lindsay and Maia
—M.M.

To Dad, Dwight, and Reece,
my three favorite farmers
—M.P.

Hi. I'm farmer Mike, and my farm is in the Central Valley of California. I always have a list of chores to do, and it seems like every time I finish one and cross it off, I have to add one more. Here's what life on my farm is like.

TO DO:

Stake the sweet peas.

Pick up 5 crates of lily bulbs and plant them.

Order 25 tons of compost.

Order melon and sunflower seeds.

Prune the apricot trees, quince trees, and almond trees.

Weed tulip beds.

Transplant a late crop of kale.

Pick 6 boxes of clementines, oranges, and grapefruit.

Cut and split the fallen walnut tree for firewood.

Income tax!

Repair the leaking skylight.

Service the tractor and bed shaper.

Change the oil in the red pick-up.

Replace the shear pin in the mower.

Set the gopher traps in the
olive trees.

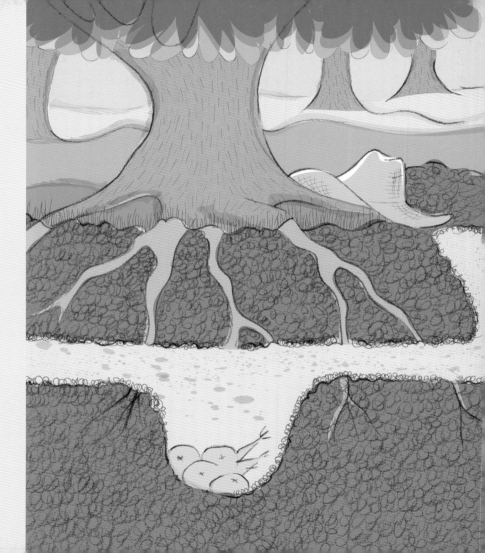

TO DO:

Weed the overgrown ranunculus beds.

Bottle 4 cases of homemade olive oil.

Start the melons and gourds in the greenhouse.

Transplant the sunflower seedlings.

Stake the lilies.

Cut back the forsythia.

Pick 60 bunches of tulips.

Plant 3000 gladiolus bulbs.

Cut and split the fallen
eucalyptus tree for firewood.

Mow the olive orchard.

Work up the flower beds in the south field.

Fix those leaking water valves.

Repair the flat tire on the truck.

Order some rubber bands and chrysanthemum cuttings.

Set the gopher traps in the
peonies.

TO DO:

Clean out the chicken coop.

Repair the broken irrigation in the orchard.

Fix the door latch to the walk-in cooler.

Replace the bait in the olive flytraps.

Restake the blown-over olive trees.

Prune the quince trees.

Order tulips, iris, and lilies
and cinnamon oil spray.

Pick 30 bunches of
sunflowers.

Harvest the tomatoes for
drying.

Arrange the flowers for a
wedding this Friday.

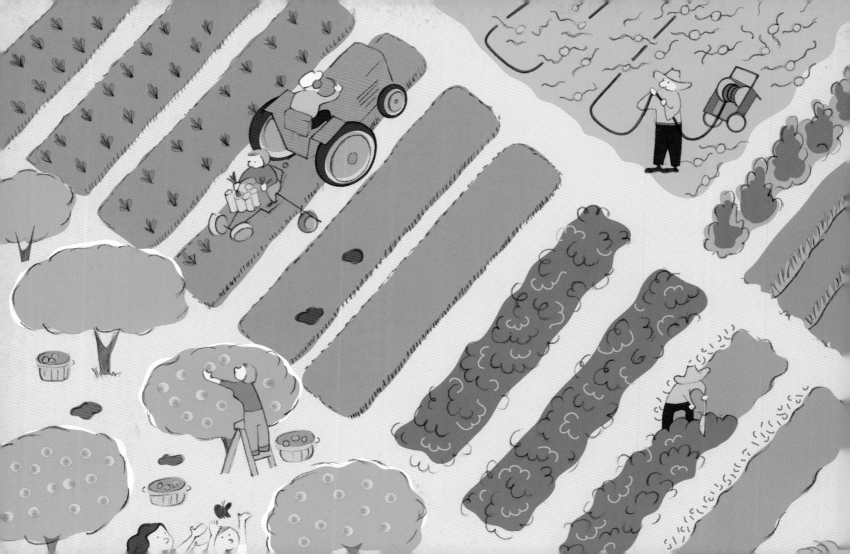

Irrigate the melon beds.

Plant out the sunflowers and zinnias. Fertilize the gerbera.

Start a late crop of marigolds and Piel de Sapo melons.

Harvest the ripe nectarines for drying.

Cut back the chrysanthemums.

Set the gopher traps in the tuberose beds.

Make some apricot jam.

TO DO:

Harvest the winter melons and move them to the barn.

Pick up some bell beans, oats, and clover seed.

Stake the chrysanthemums.

Collect the seed from the okra and tomatoes.

Save the seed from Piel de Sapo melons.

Propagate the curly willow.

Take the dead hawk in the
freezer to the zoology
museum.

Start the sweet peas.

Make 80 bouquets.

Divide the watsonia before it's too late.

Sow the pansies in the greenhouse.

Mow the old melon beds.

Order more gopher traps.

Nap.